Country School
Jerrold Beim

pictures by
LOUIS DARLING

WILLIAM MORROW AND COMPANY
New York   **1955**

5017

5017

Every morning Tony walked to
school with his brother Barry and
his sister Melody. Up a hill, around
a bend—and there under a big
maple tree stood the little country
school.

3

The little school had two rooms and two teachers. Miss Nelson was Barry's teacher and Tony liked her. She always said hello and smiled at him. *Clang! Clang!* the

schoolbell rang. Hand to his head, Tony saluted the flag with the others. *March! March!* Everyone went inside. Everyone except Tony.

Around the bend and down the hill marched Tony. He always felt sad because he wasn't old enough to go to school. There in the shade of a maple tree stood Tony's house.

"Salute the flag!" Tony played
school with his dog Taffy.

Every evening after dinner Dad opened his newspaper. "Well, listen to this!" Dad exclaimed one night. "It says that all the

little country schools around here are going to be closed. They're going to build one big new school for everybody to go to!"

"Oh, don't let them do that!" Tony cried. "I want to go to our school!" But it was true. Miss Nelson told all the children about it in the schoolyard the next day. Tony felt worse than ever. When he got home he flung himself down on the grass. He didn't even feel like playing school with Taffy.

One Sunday Dad said, "I hear they're starting to build the new school. Let's drive over and see it." They rode to the edge of the village in the family jeep. Bulldozers and excavators stood all around. They had already dug a hole big enough to swallow dozens of little schools.

Tony felt so sad he even stopped walking to school with Melody and Barry. But Dad kept driving over to see how the new school was coming along. The foundation was built. The steel frame went up. "My, it's going to be strong!" Barry said. "And big!" Melody added. "It's terrible!" said Tony.

Summer came and the children stopped going to school. But nothing stopped the building of the new school. "It has so many windows!" Barry said. "It's very modern!" Mom explained. "Well, I hate it!" said Tony.

When fall came, Barry and Melody got ready to go to the new school. Tony was glad he wasn't old enough to go. "The bus will pick you up," Mom explained to Barry and Melody. "I don't want to go on the bus. I'm scared to go to the new school alone," said Melody, and she began to cry. "Oh, dear!" Mom sighed. "Well, I'll drive you in the car for the first day."

Barry went by bus. Mom drove
Melody in the car and Tony had
to go along. The new school
looked bigger and queerer than
ever. "I'm never going to this
school," Tony said. "I don't want
to go in alone," Melody cried.
"I'll take you in," Mom said.
"Come along, Tony." She didn't
want to leave him alone.

"Why—it's kind of pretty in here!" Melody exclaimed when they reached the hall. Tony did not think so. It was filled with so many children and they were all so big! "You wait outside the door, Tony, while I take Melody to her teacher," Mom said.

Clang! Clang! The sound of a bell made Tony jump. All the boys and girls went into class-rooms and the hall was empty. Tony wondered when his mother was coming—and then suddenly

he heard the sound of someone crying. "I want my mommy!" A little girl came by, tears running down her face. "I can't find my mommy!" she wailed.

"Where is your mommy?" Tony leaned over to talk to her. She was much smaller than he. She was much too little to be going to school. "My mommy told me to wait, but I went for a drink and now I don't know where she is." She began to cry harder than ever.

"Why don't you take her to the office?" A big boy stopped in front of Tony and the little girl. "It's down at the end of the hall." Tony looked down the hall. It stretched far into the distance. He did not really want to go, but the little girl looked so unhappy. He peeked into Melody's room. Mom was still talking to the teacher. "Come on, I'll try to help you find your mother," he said.

Down, down the long hall walked Tony and the little girl. Tony tried not to show that he was scared. "What's your name?" he asked. "I'm Joan," she said. They walked and walked and then Tony saw a door with a sign on it. "Maybe this is the office," Tony said.

"Hello! I'll be with you just as soon as I fix this girl's hand." A nice lady smiled at them. "Is this the office?" Tony asked. "Oh no,

I'm the nurse," the lady said. "Go straight down the hall and you'll find the office."

"I want my mommy!" Joan started to cry again. "We'll find her!" Tony said, even though he wasn't sure they would. They walked still farther down the hall. "Let's try this door," Tony said. Joan and he walked into a big room. "This isn't the office!" Tony exclaimed. "Oh, no!" A lady smiled at him. "This is the cafeteria. All the children will have lunch here. The office is down the hall."

Down the hall! Everybody told him that. Suddenly the hall made a turn. Tony was afraid to go around the bend. He knew if he looked back he wouldn't be able to see Melody's room. He would go just a little way. He would try just one more door—that one! He opened it—and there stood Miss Nelson, his friend from the old country school.

"Tony, what are you doing here?" Miss Nelson smiled just as nicely as ever. "Joan is lost. I'm trying to take her to the office," he started to explain, but just then a man's voice came out of a box in the wall. "Welcome to your

new school, boys and girls."
"That's the principal talking from
his office," Miss Nelson whispered.
"See that third door down the
hall? That's where you want to
go."

Tony counted the doors carefully. One, two, three! He went in with Joan—and saw a man talking into a microphone. "Lunch will be at twelve o'clock in our new cafeteria. I'll see you all there." The man finished talking. He turned off the microphone. "Hello!" He smiled at Tony and Joan. "What can I do for you?"

"I found Joan," Tony said. "She lost her mother. A boy said I should bring her to the office. I'm Tony." "Well, I'm Mr. Moss, the principal," the man said. "Suppose we just announce that Joan is lost and her mother can come for her here. Why don't you announce it, young man, since you found her?" Mr. Moss lowered the microphone.

Tony backed away. "It's easy." The principal smiled. "Just say who you are and what your friend's name is. Tell her mother to come to the office for her." Tony swallowed hard but then he thought it might be fun. Mr. Moss turned on the microphone and Tony leaned forward. "Hello," he said. "I'm Tony. I found Joan. She wants her mother. We're in the office—way, *way* down the end of the long hall!"

"Joan! Joan!" A lady came rushing into the office a minute later. "I've been looking for you everywhere!" Then Mom came in too. "Why, Tony, where have you been?" "Oh, I've been all around!

I saw the nurse and the cafeteria
and Miss Nelson, and I talked on
the microphone." "I know. I was
so glad when I heard your voice,"
Mom said.

After school Barry and Melody told Tony how surprised they had been to hear his voice in their classrooms. Dad was proud when he heard about it. "You know what, Dad?" Tony exclaimed. "I think the new country school is nice. I guess I'll go there after all. Come on, Taffy, salute the flag!"